Blue's Bedtime

Published by Advance Publishers, L.C.
www.advance-publishers.com

Written by Ronald Kidd
Art layout by Niall Harding
Art composition by Mark Schroeder
Produced by Bumpy Slide Books

ISBN: 1-57973-076-0

Blue's Clues Discovery Series

Hi, there!
It's bedtime, but Blue's not sleepy!

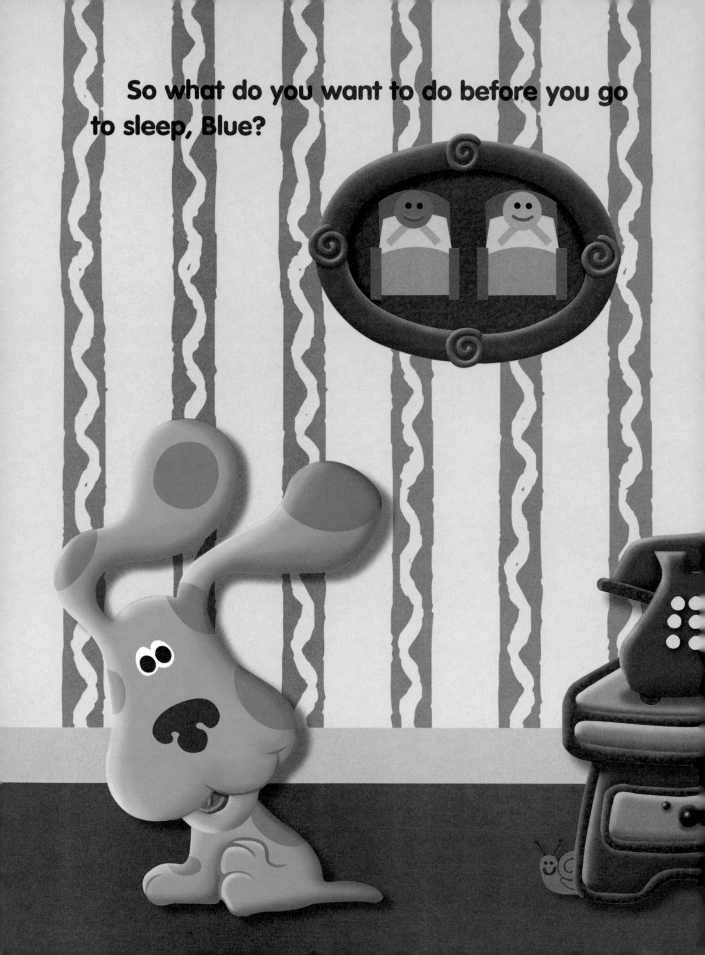

So what do you want to do before you go to sleep, Blue?

Oh! You want to play pretend. What do you want to pretend? Great! We'll play Blue's Clues to figure it out.

Maybe some of our other friends would like to play. Come on, let's go find out!

Huh? You see something? Oh, a clue! The sheet on Paprika's bed is our first clue! Good work! We're trying to figure out what Blue would like to pretend, and our first clue is a sheet. Any ideas? Hmmm. Maybe we should keep looking.

It's like counting sheep, but yummier! One soufflé, two soufflés . . . hmmm . . . I feel sleepy already!

Okay, let's go to the bedroom and see if Tickety Tock wants to play.

Oh, we thought you might want to play pretend with us.

Did you see that? Tickety fell asleep while she was talking! Oh, well, I guess we'll have to get someone else to play with us.

What's that? A clue? Oh, I see! The chair is our second clue!

Okay, we're trying to figure out what Blue would like to pretend. Yeah, I think we need to find our last clue. Let's go!

Sure, Slippery. See you tomorrow!

Now I'm starting to get tired. I sure hope we find our third clue soon!

Huh? You see a clue? Good job! Our third clue is a chair! You know what this means, don't you? It's time to go to our . . . Thinking Chair!

So our three clues are a sheet, a chair, and a chair.

What do you think Blue could want to pretend with a sheet and two chairs?

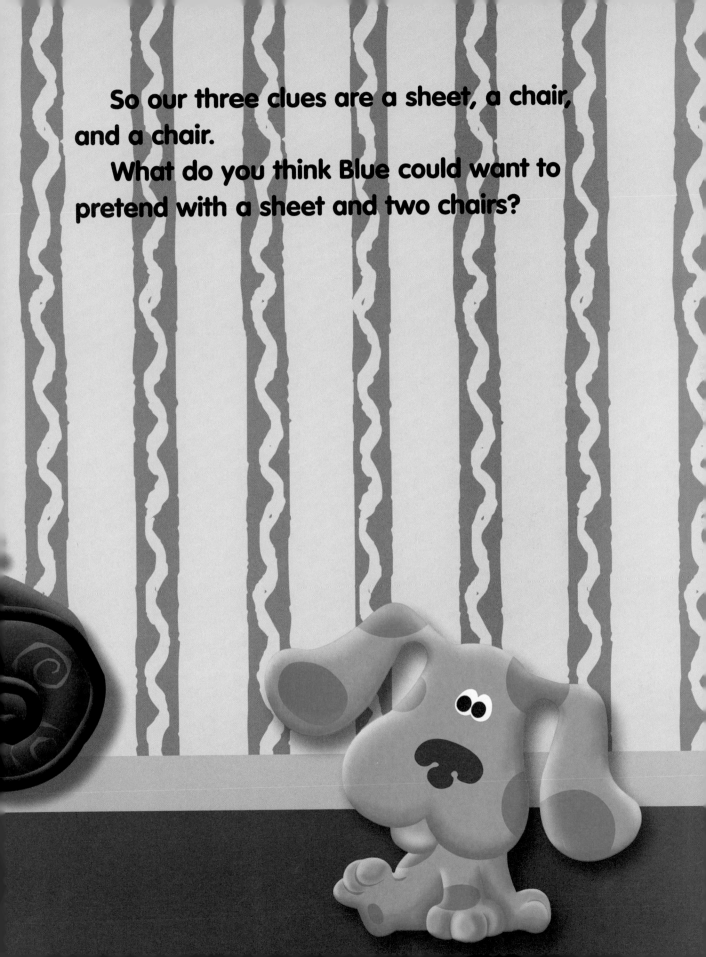

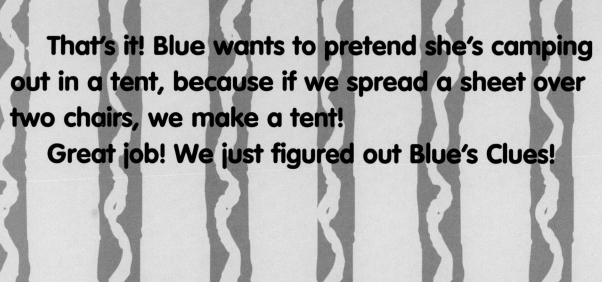

That's it! Blue wants to pretend she's camping out in a tent, because if we spread a sheet over two chairs, we make a tent!

Great job! We just figured out Blue's Clues!

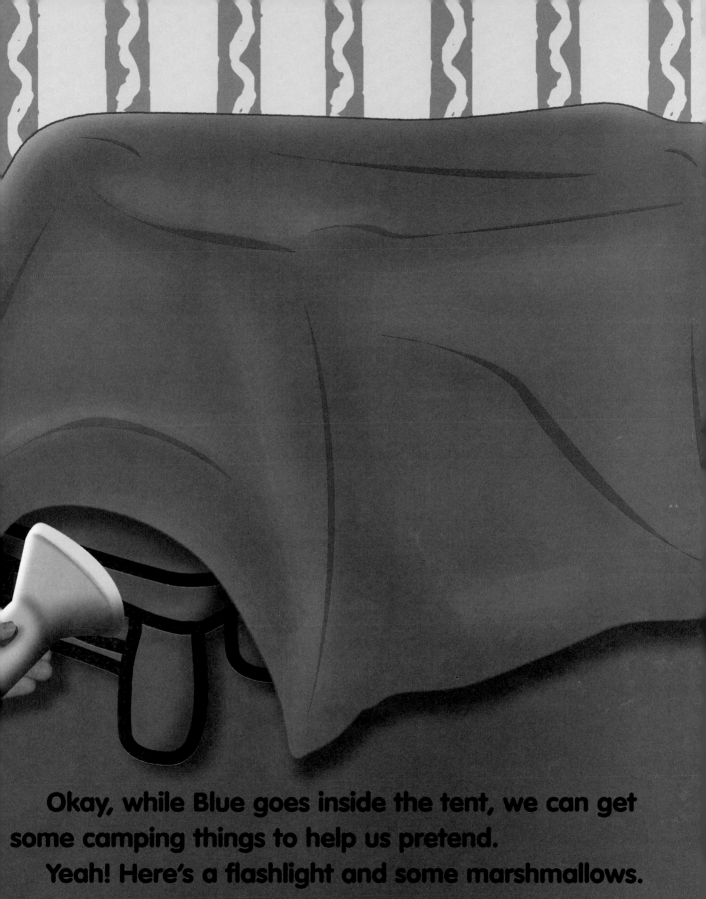

Okay, while Blue goes inside the tent, we can get some camping things to help us pretend.

Yeah! Here's a flashlight and some marshmallows.

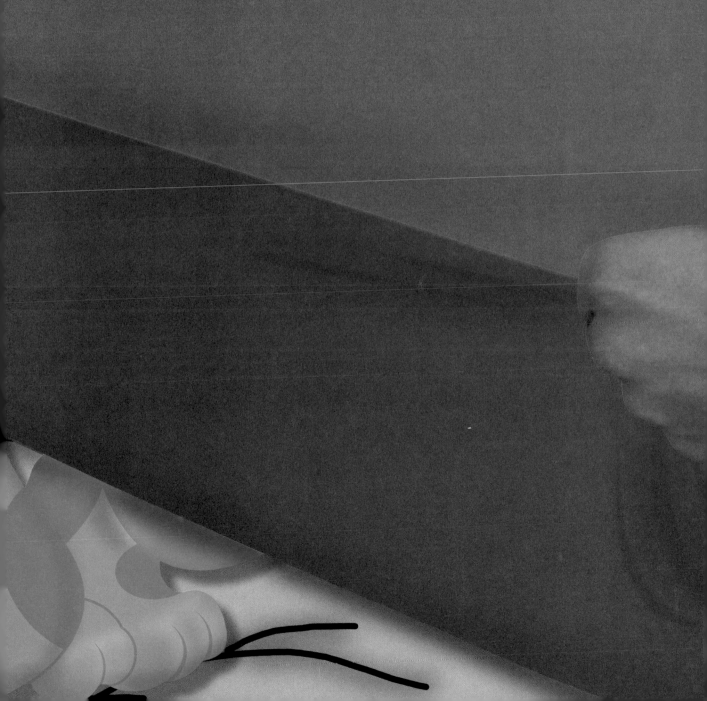

Blue, look! We've got marshmallows! Blue?

Well, what do you know—Blue fell asleep! I guess she was tired after all! You know, I'm a little sleepy myself.

Good night. And thanks for playing Blue's Clues!

BLUE'S SLIPPER SOCKS

You will need: cotton socks, cardboard, a crayon, scissors, and three-dimensional fabric paints

1. Wash and dry the socks. (Don't use fabric softener.)

2. Place a pair of your shoes on the cardboard and trace around them with a crayon.

3. Use the scissors to cut out the cardboard shoe shapes.

4. Place the cardboard shapes inside the socks so that they fill out the bottom.

5. With the cardboard shapes still in place, use the fabric paints to decorate the bottoms of your socks.

6. Let the socks dry overnight. The next day, take out the cardboard shapes and you'll have your own pair of slipper socks! (Wait three days before washing.)